A catalogue record for this book is available from the British Library

Published by Ladybird Books Ltd.
80 Strand London WC2R 0RL
A Penguin Company

4 6 8 10 9 7 5 3

Bye-Bye Blue

One sunny day on Gosling Farm, Stan was busy with his spanner. It was a tricky repair. "If I just loosen the alternator and shift it down…" muttered Stan. "Hold still, Little Red Tractor!"

Little Red Tractor couldn't help wriggling. It tickled!

"That's got it," said Stan at last. "We'd better get down to Beech Garage and get a new fan belt, just in case. Come on, Little Red Tractor. Let's go!"

"Toot! Toot!" beeped Little Red Tractor happily.

At Beech Garage, Mr Jones had brought Big Blue to Nicola and Walter for a service.

"Don't forget, Nicola," said the farmer, "after the service, he needs a jolly good spruce up. He needs to look tip-top so I can get the best price possible."

"Honk! Honk!" Big Blue didn't like the sound of that!

Walter thought the farmer was joking. "You're not thinking of selling him, are you?" he asked.

Mr Jones's reply was a big shock!

"I'm getting a new one," he said
breezily, waving a picture of a huge,
modern tractor. "It's the latest model…
the 501."

"You can't!" Nicola gasped.
"Big Blue's a great tractor!"

"He's more than just a tractor,"
added Walter.

As usual, Mr Jones wasn't listening.

"You have to move with the times," he said. "Any chance of a lift home?"

Nicola and Walter looked annoyed. They didn't feel like helping Mr Jones after what they had just heard!

As soon as the farmer had gone, Nicola and Walter tried to help Big Blue feel better.

"Don't worry, big guy, we won't let him sell you," said Walter.

Just then, Little Red Tractor and Stan pulled up. Walter told them the bad news.

Stan thought for a moment. "Hmm..." he said. "I've got a plan, but we're going to need everyone's help. Are you in?"

"You bet!" grinned Nicola and Walter.
"Honk! Honk!" blasted Big Blue.
"Toot! Toot!" Little Red Tractor agreed.

Soon everyone knew what they had
to do. Stan and Little Red Tractor set
off for Tawny Owl Wood.

"This will be the perfect spot," said
Stan when they arrived. "Hardly
anyone comes up here. Okay, Little
Red Tractor, get ready!"

Stan tied one end of a rope to a very heavy log. He fixed the other end to Little Red Tractor's tow hook.

Little Red Tractor pulled like a hero. S-l-o-w-l-y, the log inched across the track.

"Great job," smiled Stan when they had finished.

Back at Beech Farm, Mr Jones was keen to get on with the ploughing. Stumpy had zoomed over on his quad bike Nipper to lend a hand.

"But where's Big Blue?" Stumpy wondered aloud.

"Oh… er… he's on holiday," said Mr Jones, "with other tractors." He knew it sounded silly, but he didn't want Stumpy to get upset. There was work to be done!

Unfortunately, Stumpy and Nipper weren't much help. Nipper just wasn't strong enough to pull Big Blue's plough.

Mr Jones had another plan. He showed Stumpy some damp bales that needed to be pulled out into the sunshine.

"I'm not sure this is such a great idea," said Stumpy.

"Of course it is!" Mr Jones replied. He tied a rope to one of the bottom bales. Stumpy opened the throttle, and Nipper pulled with all his might.

The bale shifted, but so did all the others! They tumbled onto Stumpy and Nipper.

"Help!"
wailed Stumpy.

Just then Stan and Little Red
Tractor arrived.

"There's a tree blocking the
track through Tawny Owl Wood,"
Stan gasped. "We tried to move
it, but Little Red Tractor wasn't
strong enough. Can you help?"

"Big Blue won't have a
problem," boasted
Mr Jones. Off he hurried
to collect his tractor.

"I thought Big Blue was on holiday!" muttered Stumpy from the bales.

Stan laughed. Where had Stumpy got that idea? "You must have bumped your head!" he said. "Let's get you out of there!"

The bales were easy for Little Red Tractor to pull to one side.

Meanwhile, Mr Jones arrived at Beech Garage out of breath. He was eager to find Big Blue.

"Emergency!" he wheezed. "Big Blue and I... are the... only ones who can help!"

"Well, Big Blue's ready to go!" grinned Nicola. "Good luck!"

In no time, Mr Jones and Big Blue were speeding towards Tawny Owl Wood. Stan's plan was starting to work!

In the wood, Mr Jones quickly tied
a rope to the log and to Big Blue's
tow hook.

"Come on, Big Blue!" he shouted.
"You can do it!" called Stan, who
had just arrived with Little Red Tractor.
"Toot! Toot!" Little Red Tractor
encouraged his friend.

Stan decided it was time to tackle Mr Jones.

"It's too bad you're getting rid of him," he told Mr Jones, looking sadly at Big Blue.

"Oh no!" Mr Jones sounded horrified. "We can't break up the winning team, can we?"

"And the 501?" asked Stan.

The mighty tractor crawled forward. No problem! Big Blue and Mr Jones dragged the huge log clear.

"Well done us!" crowed Mr Jones. "What a team!"

"Honk! Honk!" blasted Big Blue proudly.

Mr Jones shook his head. "Big Blue is more than just a tractor. I don't expect you to understand, but I've really become very fond of him."

Stan couldn't help smiling. "You mean he's more like a friend than just a tractor?"

"Exactly!" agreed Mr Jones.

"Honk! Honk!" Big Blue showed how happy he was to hear that!

"Oh, I understand," said Stan. "I don't know where I'd be without my friend."

He grinned at Little Red Tractor.

"Toot! Toot!" beeped his four-wheeled friend. He felt exactly the same!